I SPY ISLAND

Meet Sue and Paul:

Sue Hendra and Paul Linnet have been making books together since 2009 when they came up with *Barry the Fish with Fingers*, and since then they haven't stopped. If you've ever wondered which one does the writing and which does the illustrating, wonder no more . . . they both do both!

For Eve – who's smart, capable and organised
so we don't have to be.

SIMON & SCHUSTER
First published in Great Britain in 2022 by Simon & Schuster UK Ltd • 1st Floor, 222 Gray's Inn Road, London, WC1X 8HB
Text and illustrations copyright © 2022 Sue Hendra and Paul Linnet
The right of Sue Hendra and Paul Linnet to be identified as the authors and illustrators of this work
has been asserted by them in accordance with the Copyright, Designs and Patents Act, 1988
All rights reserved, including the right of reproduction in whole or in part in any form
A CIP catalogue record for this book is available from the British Library upon request
978-1-4711-9630-0 (PB) • 978-1-4711-9632-4 (eBook) • Printed in Italy • 10 9 8 7 6 5 4 3 2 1

I SPY ISLAND

SUE HENDRA
PAUL LINNET

BOOK vs. SHARK

SIMON & SCHUSTER

London   New York   Sydney   Toronto   New Delhi

In the middle of the ocean,

miles from anywhere,

was a happy little island who loved to play.
"I spy with my little eye . . .

something beginning with 'S' . . ."

"Oh, Island," said Bird. "It's not the sea AGAIN, is it?"
"No," said Island.
"It's not the sea, actually. It's a . . . 'S . . . omething' and it's just washed up on my chin!"

"Let's go and see what it is," said Treasure Chest, excitedly.

"But what if it wants to eat me?" panicked Bottle.

"I don't think that's very likely," said Bird, calmly.

"What if I want to eat it," asked Banana.

"No one is eating anybody," said Treasure Chest, firmly, as it helped the visitor up.

"Hello! I'm a book!" said the book.
"And I'm very pleased to meet you!"

"Ooooo, a book!" cried Glove. "And books mean stories.
I LOVE stories! What is your story about?"
"I'll show you!" the book said, proudly.

But when it threw open its pages . . .

they were empty!

"My story! It's gone!" cried Book.
"It must have washed off
in the sea!"

Book was horrified.
The friends were concerned.

"Can you remember anything about your story?"
asked Island.
"No," said the little book, "I really can't."

"Try not to worry," said Island.
"Perhaps if we tell you OUR stories,
it might help you to remember yours?
Now, who wants to start?"

"I've got a story!" said Bottle. "It's about a factory where lots of bottles are made, and they all look the same but they are not the same.

One is special and is chosen to carry an important message across the sea . . ."

"I've got a better one," said Banana.
"It's about a banana that eats lots of yummy things.

On Monday, it eats a doughnut,
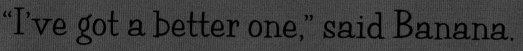

on Tuesday,
it eats two
cupcakes,

on Wednesday,
it eats three
sprouts . . . "

"I think we get the idea, Banana,"
said Bird. "What about you, Glove?
Do you have a story?"

"My story is a sad story.
It's about a glove that had a glove twin,
but the string that held them together snapped
and they never saw each other again . . ."

Telling this story made
Glove a bit gloomy,
so the friends gave it
a cuddle.

" . . . but then it found lots of wonderful
new friends!" continued Glove, smiling.

"Tell us your story, Treasure Chest!" said Bird, so Treasure Chest told its tale of kings and queens.

And it was a grand story of riches, splendour and adventure on the high seas . . .

Finally, it was Bird's turn.
"My story began in a nest," said Bird.
"It was very cosy in the nest, but then
I had to learn how to fly.

I wasn't very good
at it to start with.
It was scary!

But then I got
the hang of it.

And I loved it SO much
that I flew all the way
here to the island.

When everyone had finished,
Book sighed a big sigh.
"You're all so kind," it said.
"These are wonderful stories . . .

. . . but none of them feel like MY story."

And off Book went to sit by the water's edge.

"Only you can know what your story is," said Island, gently.

"That's the problem," said Book, sadly. "I just don't know."

And Book was feeling SO sad that it didn't notice a stirring and a bubbling in the water below . . .

"Hello, little book," said an ENORMOUS shark.

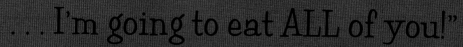

". . . I'm going to eat ALL of you!"

"But WHY?" the friends shouted together.
"Why do you want to eat us?"

"'Cos I'm bored. There's nothing to do. I swim about. I eat stuff. I see a fish. I see another fish. I'm bored, bored, bored, bored,

bored."

And with that, the shark opened its huge mouth and its sharp white teeth glistened in the sunlight.

The friends huddled together. What or who could save them now?!

To everyone's surprise, Book took a step forward.

"BORED?! But how can you possibly be bored?

There are so many wonderful things to see, places to visit, things to do – so many exciting things to learn about.

The world is an AMAZING place!
There are . . .

Astronauts
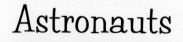

and Boomerangs,
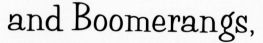

Cactuses and

Dinosaurs,

Electricity

and Flowers

and Gravity

and Hats!

And then there's Ice,

Jam Sandwiches

and Karate

and Llamas,

Marshmallows (oh, now THEY'RE yummy)

and the Northern Lights, gosh, they're SO beautiful . . ."

Book paused for breath. Its new friends were stunned. "Book! That was amazing! YOU'RE amazing! And you're not a story book . . . you're a book filled with facts from A to Z and that makes you an encyclopedia!"

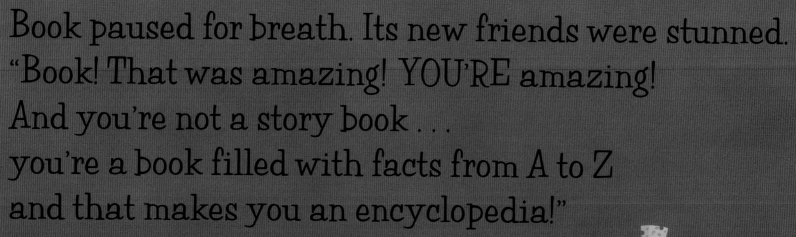

"I think you're right," gasped Book, "I am! And I'm still a story book, because an encyclopedia tells the story of EVERYTHING!"

Just then, the shark cleared its throat and everyone turned to look.

It was deadly serious.
It scrunched up its face,
bared its teeth, and:
"GRRRRRRR . . . ,